AFTERLIFE VOL. 1

RAW VERSION

YOGENDRA NIKALE

Copyright © Yogendra Nikale
All Rights Reserved.

mark
" you are god, you could have put mme here.
god
"when i made this world i made rules for myself too. if i dont follow
my own rule so iam not god.

title : afterlife
written by : yogendra nikale.
one 10 year old boy named mark with thick sungrases and braces on
his teeth. entering the school primises.
he is walking in on the floor and everyone is with their friends and
talking to each other but no one notices him. he is alone and lonely.
one boy pushes him and he falls.
the boy : ohh i didnt even notice. you are there. actually no one
notices you.
mark gets up and starts walking towards his classroom.
cut to
a new boy enters the school. the teacher intruduces the new boy. the
boy is black and has crooked teeth.
teacher :heres a new boy in our classroom. who wants to be his
friend. [the new boy waves every one points at mark]
teacher : ohh mark. looks like you a got a new friend.
the boy sits beside mark.
the boy : hi. im henry.
mark : hi. im mark.
henry : i know.
mark : but how?
henry : teacher just took your name.
mark : ohh, your too smart.
henry : and your too dump.
mark looks at he says im just kidding.

mark looks at mona and she is fancy for simon. they both are holding hands and henry watches them.
henry : looks like the girl of your dreams is with someone else.
cut to
teacher watching simon and mona says " you little love birds get a closer look at me when im teaching you.
henry : look like they are the romeo annd juiet of the classroom and with a oger in their story.
mark again gives him a weired look.
cut to
ssports day of the school runners have to give wooden stick to other runner before he start running.
mark is in simon's team. the race starts and simon is supose to give the stick to the mark. and then mark will run further towards mona and then mona will continue the race.
simon starts running towards mark.
henry is in other team and stannding next to mark.
henry : this is your chance to be friends with mona. you have to give it to her right.
mark : [watches at mona and says yeah]
henry : wait i'll help you, [and removes marks his glasses from his face and throws away from the field and a guy passing by maintaining the crowd with his wistle steps on it by mistake and doesnt notice], this wont distract your run.
mark : but i cant see.
henry : you want to see who. just run like hell.
simon comes with thewooden stick and gives it to mark. there was difficulty for mark to catch the stick due to his blurry vision and he take the stick and runs.
mark runs ofcourse from the race iin full speed due to his blurry vision.

mark is ruuning towards the guy and he is about to dash the guy with whistle.

the guy watches him and jumps upwards so that mark would go from undr his legs.

mark running in full speed towards the guy, the guy jumps and his head hits the balls of the guy with the wistle and mark dashes into the fence.

cut to

henry is getting the medal for the race and mona and simon looking i anger towards injured mark. and mark hides his face.

cut to

at night mark kisses the picture of the mona takes the blanket on his head and sleeps.

cut to

the sunrise and mark removes his blanket from his head and he is teen age now. wears his glasses and watches the teen age picture of mona and gets out of his bed.

cut to

mark reached the college and he meets henry.

henry : hey mark, i got this for you. [gives him a folded poster.]

mark opens the fold and watches the poster its thee pamela andreson hot picture.

mark : what the fuk is this.

henry : you dont have a girl, so you might use it.

mark ; you dont have a girl too henry.

henry : i have used it, [shows a dried stain of sperm on the picture] look here's the proof.

mark throws away the poster and says "what the fuck is wrong with you"

henry stares at mona : actually what the fuck is wrong with her.

they both starts watching that mona is ahving a fight with simon.

mark : i htink they are having a fight.
henry : lets get little closer.
they come closer and mona says's "its over simon. its over between you and me"
henry : this is your chance to get your girl of dreams.
mark : what do i do.
henry : tell her, how you feel about her. the flame in your heart is from your childhood.
mark : i cant, i panic when ever i speak to any girl.
henry : so write it down, i will give you the letter.
mark looks at him and he decides to write a leter.
they both in the library. mark starts writting the letter.
henry : do it fast, you may loose the day.
mark : i have started from the begining. [the librarian shhsshs them]
mark starst whispering to henry : i have started from the begining. let me recolect my memories.
henry : just tell her you are fancy for her.
mark : alright its done. [henry snatches the letter]
while going towards mona he makes some changes with his pen. and mark is watching it.
mona was busy reading a book. henry goes from her back and keeps the letter and the desk and walks away. mona doesnt notice him.
henry comes back to mark and sits beside him and says mission accomplish. "mission accomlish"
mark : what were you writing in the letter.
henry : what sheat did yoou write, there were spelling mistakes man. you can can afford mistakes in resume but not in love letter.
mark : thank you henry you are my true friend.
henry : now look over there she is about to see your letter.
mona was packing all his stuff and she watches her right to take the books. she finds a letter. and she looks around and starts reading.

henry : alright then show has started, i got to make a move. i hhave a science project.[henry moves from there]
mark keeps watching her and she is impressed by his lettter and she kisses the letter.
and mark smiles watching it.
mark comes towards the science lab searching for henry.
mark opens the door and he watches his lletter down. he picks it up.
he hears sound.
mona : really, you loved me from my childhood. and you spoke. i really never knew.
mark turns left saying yeah and he watches. henry is fucking mona on the table.
and mona is speaking : i really love you. boy. i will never leave you alone.
henry looks at him and laughs. hehehehehe.
mona : who is it, who are you laughing at. [mona was about to look at him]
mark gets back and hides behind the wall and reads the letter. he notices his name is been erased and its written henry at the end of the letter.
cut to
mark throws the letter and goes out of there.
cut to
mark in the road walking and he watches a magazine cover page.
there was a sexy picture of a model.
he takes the magazine and run
cut to
he throws his girlfriends picture in the dustbin.
mark lies on the bed watching magazine and starts jerking off. [top shot, and camera pan and tto the same shot from the top but mark 40 yeaars old. and this he is having a smart phone in his hand]

cut to

the model from the phone showing her tits. and mark jerking off.

cut to

mark is working in a electronic shop. sitting quietly on the stool. selling an electronic toy and a big poster of the toy on the counter. and he watches the other guys are selling phones and others products.

cut to

the boss of the electronic shop is in his cabin siiting on his desk and mark is there to answer him about the sales.

the boss : this is the third week in line. you havent sold a single peice. i have to cut you down.

mark : this is because. you gave a product which is out dated. no one buys a eltronic robot. who repeatedly says " im the future and im comming to get you"

mark : everyone is into video games, snapchats and lot of cool stuff.

mark opens the window annd wacthes a booy kickking the robot poster and says "old school" .

mark shows him to his boss the boy kicking

mark : you seee that, you gave me a wrong product to sell.

mark shows his boss the other guys. look they are having the right product.

the boss : you see those guys overthere. there is one thing in common in them. they are happpy in what they are doing. look how they greet people and you boy its been 20 years your working here, i never saw that in you. you always gave a poor prformance. why is it so.

mark : i dont know what your talking about.

the boss : you see that girl over there. [shows him stella hony potting his clients.] why she is so good at this.

mark : because she always had good products, like phone, tv and

video games.
the boss looks at her tits and says "ohhh her products"
boss : no its not her products, she knows a way get her job done. i
bet if she is selling the toy, she will increase the sales.
mark : i will leave this job immideatly , i bet she wont.
cut to
stella in robo bikini. and a electric gun in the hand and selling the
product.
there is a long queue to buy from her.
stella talking like a robot : im the future and im coming to get you
[and doing the gun actions]
one kid point at robot and say's to his father : dad i want one of
those.
father watching at stell's tits and say's mee too son mee too.
the boss shows mark stella is doing the business. mark stares him
and her on the floor.
cut to
mark gathering all his stuff from the locker and putting it in a box.
stella comes there and watches mark removing his stuff.
stella : hey, mark. i just came to know. you are leaving because of me.
mark : no, thats not it. im no use here. actually im no use to everyone.
mark emptied his locker and starts walking. stella hold his hand and
stops him.
stella : hey mark. i nevver wanted this.
mark : dont blame yourself. its just me. good for nothing and now
unemployed.
stella : i dont think so. when there is a end. after that there is a new
begining.
mark : yeah, begining of staying hungry.
stella holds him tight : maybe i wont llet you stay hungry.
mark : i dont need money from you.

stella : i mean to say i wont let you stay hungry. [she kisses him] now
do you know. what i meant.
mark looking her in shock.
stella : my husband lives out in weekdays. maybe we can look each
other tonight and decide who is more starving.
mark breathing heavy "yeah"
stella : dont make me wait too long. [camera pann to the boss and he
is watching them and listening]
cut to
mark jumping in his room andshouting and running.
mark : after 40 fucking years.
and dancing in the house and saying no more jerking off.
cut to
mark getting his nose hair removed from a mchine and he watches
hair on his his chest coming out side from his chest.
cut to
mark has removed his shirt and his chest is all covered with hair. and
raises his arm to see his pits in the mirror. there are 15 inchhes long
hair in his pits.
mark starts removing from a hair remover machine.
the load of hair in the house.
cut to
mark is all cleaned his chest hair. and trying different shirts.
and watches time. its 9.
mark : i got to quit playing around.
mark gets dressed and wears a perfume and goes out.
as he goes out of the house. a car comes towards him.
cut to
[long shot] everyone on the street shoulting. and gathered ner the
accident.
cut to.

mark opens his eyes and he watches everything black.
mark cleans his sunglasses. he watches no wall, no other colour.
mark : where the fuck am i.
mark : hello, anybody here. helloo.
one guy : hey im here.
mark : where. [mark looking around and cant find anyone.]
mark : i can hear you but i cant see you. where are you.
mark starts walking.
the guy : can you give little direction. east, west or north south.
mark : i know nothing. i cant tell where i am. just try to reach my
voice and i will try yours. and keep talking.
the guy : what is this place.
mark : i dont know. i was headed to meet someone. and suddenly
flashlight came and i landed here. what about you.
the guy : i was flying in my helicopter and there was a bad weather.
and i dont remember after that. i opened my eyes and i woke up
here.. well i can see you.
mark : where.
the guy : look on your side. [mark turns the other side]
mark : ohh i see you.
cut to
they both starts walking together
mark : what you think where are we.
the guy : no wall, all black. our disapearance i think its the aliens.
mark : look there are people, maybe they know where are we.
far he watches a queue entering into the gate. mark walks twards
them.
mark tries to enter the gate and people from the queue say's "get in
line"
the guy with starts to fight with the gate keeper.
guy : what the fuck is this, where the fuck am i.

the gate keeper : get in line you get all your answers.
tthe crowd : yeah get in line. we aint fool.
the guy catches the collar of the gate keeper and says's " i need some answers now"
the gate keeper : boys i need a little help.
two huge guys from the gate stands up.
mark watchng them : ohhh fuck look at the size of that guys
one bouncer picks the guy and starts walking at the end of the line.
and the second one comes for the mark.
mark walks back and say's " i will walk from here thank you. "
mark watches there is a long queue.
mark starts walking to reach the end of it. and he watches all are injured people. and stabbed people.
mark gets in the line.
mark : what iis this?
the guy in front of him : no, one know. looks like its some kind of hospital. the last thing o remember i was in my bathroom . and i oppened my eyes and i got into line to check what is going on.
mark : your head is bleeding.
the guy in front : nah! it might be the shampoo.
mark : no its blood.
the guy in front touches his head and shows him. "but its not paining "

people coming and getting in line behind mark.
mark : this got be somekkind of joke.
the guy behind mmark : i think its a halloween party. mght be a new club. look everyone are in costumes.
mark watches everyone are in bloody costumes. and he watches forward.
cut to
in the queue don stepped on the foot of don 2, as don 2 was behind

and they started fighting near the gate.
don 2 : hey fuck face watch where your going.
don : who the fuck do you think your talking too. [and starts
searching his gun n his jacket and cannot find it]
don : where the fuck is my gun? i dont know whats happening over
here. but wait until my men arrive, you are a dead man.
don : i think i got my gun [he gets his gun and shoots]
don 2 falls down.
the watchman : yeah, yeah. move forward. he is a dead guy now.
don enters the gate.
don 2 gets up saying im alive im alive.
the watchman looks at him and watches up.and says "i hate this job"
cut to
don enters one employee asks don to step on the verification booth.
don steps. the machine take his name.
machine : [machine scans him] mr. johny francheska. verified.
don: how does the machine knows my name.
the booth guy : step further sir.
don : no, you teell me first. whats going on. i havent used this name
for years.
the booth guy : i said step down mate. there is a big queue.
don : no, im not. im ggoing back.
the booth guy to himself : when will you people understand.
the booth guy on the radio : alright, we got a trouble make. [presses
the red button next to him]
the don falls down in a hole. and there comes a deemon with a big
dick and oiling his dick.
cut to
the booth guy to himself : let me check your deeds.
the machine says : killed in a gun fight.
there is scale weight machine of good deeds and bad deeds

the bad deeds wwight is more and on the screen it comes red.
the booth guy : well you are at the right place.
new guy comes there. : hey dude. i can take it from here.
the booth guy : thank god you came. seriouly i was waiting when my shift gets over.
new guy : so whats the status.
the booth guy : hardly you are getting any guy going in the blue. well people make their own choice.
cut to
the guy before mark reaches till the front gate.
the guy goes inside.
the guy stands in the verification booth.
the machine scans him : mr. bill white. verified.
new guy : you may step down sir.
the deeds calculator starts and there comes weight on the red and blue scale stimulator. and the blue weights more.
and on the screen there comes blue.
new guy : you may go in the blue door sir.
mr. bill goes inside the blue door.
the new guy : checks on screen.
the machine answers : reason of death fall down on bath tub and hit his head.
the gate opens and mark enters.
the new guy : step on the verification booth.
mark : stands on it.
the machine scans him
the machine : mr. mark whisley. verified.
the new guy : you may step down.
mark : what is this all about.
the new guy : just a moment, all your confusions will be cleared.
the new guy starts the deed calculator.

and there is no weight on the blue.
the new guy watches him : what are you.
and one weight on blue falls and 2 on red falls. and the screen says
red.
the new guy : you may get in the red door sir.
mark starts walking towards the spooky red door.
as mark enters the door. the new starts checking his details.
the machine : death by an accident.
new guy : let me check your sins
the new guy starts checking his sins
the machine answers. : his sins were masterbeating and kissing a
married woman. he was about to have sex but he died in an accident.
the new guy laughs and calls on his phone.
you guys have no idea. who have just enetered. this guys sins are
gonna make laugh the entire hell. wait im sending you the details [the
new guy send his videos from his phone]
cut to
mark watches a black gate and background is all smmokey and evil.
mark gets in.
red coloured girls opens the gate : welcome.
one girl : is he the one.
other girl : yeah he is the one.
they starts laughing.
mark turns back and looks at them they stops laughing.
mark : nice costume.
the red girls sending messages
evvery guard in the hell gets the messages.
cut to
mark enters the hell and everything is fiery.
mark to himself : this is some fine set up. [watches a guy with horns
on his head] they really have some nice costumes.

mark gets in line again
mark : one more queue. how big is this place.
the guy with the horns pushes a guy. "move forward fast"
as mark comes near the horn guy. he starts laughing.
the horn guy sccreams : look whos here the jerker.
every guard starts laughing.
mark starts walking.
one guard starts immittaing of jerking off and kissing.
mark watches it and walks further.
devil in his cabin.
devil playing dart games and a man is rotating. on the board.
devil's friends are sitting around the table and watching.
devil : come on im bored of this crap.
devil's friends : its your job.
devil : i know, the same old punishment. nothing new. i'll take the day
off and you guys punish them my book. [devil shhows them the book
from his desk]
one guard comes running.
guard : sir you wont beleive who is next.
devil : donalld trump.
guard : no. a jerker.
devil gets in seat : all right send him in.
devil gets in his chair.
devil : all right everyone ready send him in.
mark enters.
mark : whats going on here.
devil : im here to punish you for your sins.
mark : punish me for what.
devil : for jerking off for 15 thousand 7 hundred and 94 times.
one guy from the chair laughs. the guy next to him makes him quite.
mark : what are you saying. what kind of joke is this. and where am i.

devil snaps his finger and turns into the model from the internet video.

the model : maybe this will remind you.

mark : what the fuck, what kind of magic is this. how did you ......

model snaps his finger turn back to devil

devil : so, do you deny this.

mark : yes. absolutely.

devil : all right then, is this you.

devil turns on the video on his big screen.on that screen. there are videos of mark jerking on his bed.

mark watches it.

mark : holly sheat. [gets shocked watching it]

everyone in the room starts laughing.

cut to

the video of mark watching the video on mobile and jerking. [close up shot]

cut to

mark jerking in the bathroom.

cut to

mark : ohh sheat, shut it, shut it [ggoes near the big screen and tries to turn the big screen off.

the guy on the rolling dart board is also laughing. and everyone in the room too.

devil turn ooff the video.

devil : so tell me is this you.

mark : what the fuck is happening here. you rigged cameras in my house. now i get it. this is some kind of prank show.

mark : alright you got me, noww let me go home.

devil : you still dont get it do you. im the devil, lucifer. the lord of all demons.

maark : come on now you are taking it too far budy.

one demon from the roundtable gets up in anger. : watch your mouth you scoundrel. beware who you are talking too.

devil to the demon : relax take it easy. he is new.

mark : he is the devil. and im gonna get punished for my sins and who are you asmodeaus.

demon points at a guy : no he is asmodeous.[asmodeous is oiling his dick and says hi] im valek.

mark : and i am george cloney [mark starts walking outside and devil flickers his fingers watching him]

and mark falls down in a hole. and he keeps on falling and he watches people are getting punished around him. and he was about to fall in lava.

as mark falls down. he falls in the same room.

mark : what did you just do to me. [he looks around and everyone smiling at him] i guess you are telling the truth.

the hanged guy : you are right. deviil throws the knife on the dart.

devil gets up : welcome to hell.

the camera pans and people are getting punished and long shot pan of the hell.

cut to

one guard put mark in a cell.

mark : please i will never jerk off again. i promise. atleast tell me how did i die.

the television start in his cell.

mark sit on his bed.

mark : ohh a television. [shouts] is this realy a prison.

the television starts and the tittle comes the mask man.

mark : ohhh the mask man. superhero movie, i have never seen this before.

the movies was a parody porn.

mark watching it starts getting horny.

devil and his friends are watching it from his cabin.
devil : wait for it.
mark starts unzipping his pant.
devil : yes, he is going for it.
mark puts his hand in his pants and finds no dick.
mark : what the fuck [he couldnt find his dick] where is my dick. [yells] where is my dick.
mark opens watches in his pant and there is no dick.
mark shouts ahhhhhhhh!
devil and his friends laughs in his cabin.
cut to
mark is shoulting outside the cage. and devil behind. mark looks at the devil and shouts and devil snaps his finger. and says"shut it will you "
devil starts walking and mrk follows him.
devil :. your making me sleepy. screams are my lullaby.
mark speaking with devil and there is no voice.
devil : now i dont like sileince either.
devil looks at mark and watches he is speaking but there is noo voice.
devil : ohh im sorry,[he flickers is fingers and mark's voicecomes back]
mark : what the fuck has happened tomy dick.
devil : like jerking dont you. here.[flickers his hand] here's your dick back.
mark gets his dick back.
mark puts hand in his pants to check his dick.
mark : ohh my goodness i got it back.
mark removes his glasses and wears it.
mark : is it mine.
mark : why is my glasses are not working.
devil sitting in a couch smoking.

devil : all your injuries goes away here,
mark : i see a man crippled guy over there. [points at a guy walking
with the help of crutches]
devil : that guy, he would have been a football player. very strong
kicks. but he used his legs to kicking people.
shots of the guy kicking
in office to his employees "i told you guys to get the job done" kicks a
guy who was sitting in his desk working on a laptop. and he falls.
kicking his servants, "i told you get the pool cleaned there's a party"
after the kick the servant fallls in the pool.
the guy was sleeping with his wife and his wife puts a hond on him
and he wakes up. so while his wife sleeping he kicks his wiife saying
"get off me " and the wife fells down the bed. and his wife]
devil : so he is punished here. god gave him powers but he misused it.
and landed here.
devil : you see the only guy can harm here is me. [devil snaps his
fingers and his eye's disapear]
mark : ohh my eyes, my eyes. i got it, i got it.
devil snaps his fingers again. mark gets his eyes back.
mark : i'm here because of jerking off. [comes near the couch.]
devil snaps and a bean bag comes and mark is seated in that bag.
mark gets shocked after this act.
mark : so im here because of jerking off.
devil : no. thats not it.
mark : then what.
devil snaps his finger and he gets a drink in his hand.
devil : why dont you have a drink first. refresh yourself and refresh
your memory.
mark was taking his glass closer towards his mouth and he watches
himself kissing stella on the top of the glaass.
mark : alright i got it. i kissed a woman so what.

devil : not any woman. a married woman. it comes in adultry. one of the ten commandments.
mark : it was just a kiss
devil : but its a sin.
mark : but i didnt harm anyone.
devil : but your act didnt helped you either.
mark : what do you mean.
devil : well let me show you how it works.
devil snaps his fingers and there comes the deed calculator.
devil : you must be familiar with with this.
mark : yeah i saw it before entering here. what is it.
devil : itss your deeds, this stimulator decides where you are gonna go.
mark : i have always been a good guy. you can check it.
devil : i know, you always abeyed your parents thats why its little blue, thats the onlly good acct you ever did.
[visuals a old man lifting his lugage and mark not helping him. blindman waiting to cross and mark not helping him. mark crossing by the beggar and not giving him anything.]
devil : but did you help anyone cross the street. or did some kind of charity. or any selfless act. you will always get an apportunity to do good. but you didnt.
mark stares at him.
mark : but it doesnt mean that im a bad guy.
devil : i have seen bad ass motherfucker enjoying in heaven.
[visuals the weight stimulator fill with red weights]
devil : but all their sins are lifted due to their good deeds [blue weight on the stimmulator increases and the red gets lifted]
mark looks down in tension
mark : but how did i die.
devil : son i like you, but i got a big job to do.

cut to
a sinner sleeping in his room and a water drop falls on his head and
he wakes up.
he looks around and he watches there is no one around the
houseand the window is smahing on the wall due to the wind.
sinner gets up closes the window. and goes to sleep again.
again the window starts banging. sinner gets up and watches there is
a scary woman outside the window. the sinner gets scared. and she
disappears.
he looks at his right there is a boy with spoon and fork. he gets
scared and falls down the bed.
he gets up and watches. around there is no one. but there is a
pentagram on his bed. he gets more scared.
and suddenly from all aound his house ghosts comes. from the
sealings, from the floor. from the window from the wall. and he is
watching everyone and he faints. zoom out
cut to
devil in his cabin watching.
devil laugh : bravo, bravo. [and claps]
and every ghost from the screen watching im and bending down after
their performance.
devil : i loved this one. hey boy you were incredible.
the boy : thank you your highhness.
devil : where is the sealing guy.
the guy from the sealing upside down. : im here sir.
devil : excelent job. mind blowing performance.
the sealing guy : thak you your highness.
devil : where the guy under the bed.
one ghost : there is no one sir.
devil : put someone there. will you. and make it more scary.
everyone answers : yess your highness.

devil : and where is the witch.

with from the the window.

devil : dont forget your my favourite.

the witch smmilles and sends a flying kiss. and the devil acts he takes it and touches his heart.

devil looks at mark : ha ha did you like it.

mark : i guess you love torturing people.

devil : not just any people. when this fellow was alive. [visuals of the man on earth.]

devil : he used too fool people around him that evvery full moon he does the rituals and devil gets inside him. he scared the sheat out of them. [visual the sinner is doing voodoo rituals in the out at night and people from their house are watching him. and next day in the mmorning, people find the pentagram candles and blood on the floor of that spot.]

devil : he used to take money from people. for the saftey of their children. or else he would eat them. such a big ppossy by my name. [visuals of sinner taking money from the parents in their house and children watching them and the sinner smiles at them and the children hide]

cut to

mark and devil walking in hell.

mark : so how did he died.

devil : one night he was doing a fake ritual and i had enough of him. one night he was doing his retuals. [visuals sinner doing the rituals outdoor and devil comes in front of him. and devil say's "did you call me"]

devil : he died in a instant heart attack. [visual dying sinner]

mark : so why did anyone record his video. complained he would have been prisoned.

devil : there were no cameras in the year 1855

mark gets shocked.
devil : i did nothing, he called me. so just visited him. even though im not allowed there.
mark : but there are sayings that people get possesed by demons.
devil laughs : do you really think, i will leave all my work and posses someone.
mark : but i have seen people getting possesed. and there are exorcism. that means it all fake. [visual possess shhot and priest doing exorcism]
devil : i didnt say so.
mark : then.
devil : the souls which do not enter the gate of judgement. and run away. [visuals of souls running from the gate or not entering the gate.]
devil : they keep on wondering in the dark and sometimes the fear of a person opens a portal from the darkness . and the souls they atract the light of life and hence people get possesed. [visuals wodering in the dark and atracked to light and a mann gets poossesed]
devil : the souls in the dark, are neither from heaven and neither from hell. they are not even alive neither dead. they are just lost souls.
they both are walking and don comes running towards them saying ohhh my ass my ass.
the devil snaps his fingers annd the don disapears goes back to same demon. and the demon's dick is lept. watching him it gets errect and he smiles.
don : what the fuck.
cut to.
mark looks in front of him. ther was a pool of white mud.
mark : whats this.
devil : you must be knowing that chick over there.

mark watches her

the girl says hi mark

mark recognizes that he has jerked off watching her picture and cummed on her picture. [vision mark jerking and and cumming on her picture]

mark : ohh sheat.

devil : yeah that's the one.

mark : how did she get here.

devil : her sin is very intersting.

the model i doing nude photo shoot.

the cameraman to the model : you are gonna make lot of people cum baby.

model : i hope so.

devil : and here she is all covered in cum.

mark : this is cum.

devil : yeah, what you thought liquid soap.

mark : yuk lets go from here. [they starts walking]

mark watches a guy.

mark : hey there is a guy too.

devil : yeah from the gay magazine.

the guy from the cum licks cum from his hand and says hi to mark.

mark : eww.

devil : you want to see the porn video section.

mark : no thats enough. i have seen enough. what happens to their soul. are they stuck here for ever.

devil :no, they do their time here and they reincarnate. but not into humans, animals or insect. according to their sin, whorst the sins whorst they become.

sinners were walking with the log on their back and they are chained to and devil. and mark walking by and the guard watching their que. one sinner disapears. and the other one staring.

cut to

on earth the sinner has become a mosquito and sits on a human body.

the human kills the mosquito by smashhing it.

cut to

the sinner comes back to the hell and starts walking in the same line.

the other sinner : let me guess a moquito again.

the sinner : i didnt even chance to drink some blood.

the other sinner laughs.

cut to

mark : i need a way out. i cannot do this. i dont want to turn into a reptile or a mosquito.

devil looks at him.

devil : come lets have a drink

cut to

a sexy girl making a drink and mark s watching her assets. devil is smoking hukka.

giving a drink to mark.

mark smiles at the girl and the girl smiles back at him. she is having fangs like a vampire.

mark gets scared and looks at devil.

devil : she is a beauty isnt she.

mark looks tensed to devil.

devil : come on relax. this is the end of your world not mine. have i treated you badly.. i dont treat this way to anyone. whhy im treating you as a guest. because you didnt harm anyone. i like you.your a good chaerything happened so fast. i didnt even know.

devil : that your going to die. no one knows when they are gonna die. it just happens. so you have to keep doing the good work. but now its too late for that.

mark : yeah. i will do it. from now.

devil : its too late. boy. i cant help you. the only thing i can do is i wont punish you. and unless and untill your punishment isnt over you wont reincarnate.so you will be stuck here for ever. together we will have a ball here.

mark : i dont want to stay here. i know the value of life now. i have done nothing. good and evil. the sins which i did i didnt even know they were sins. i want to enjoy life again. i want to live again.

mark : there might be some way. come on your the devil. there is always a way.

devil stares at him : i think there is one way.

cut to

devil is taking mark to a dark place. like dungeons.

mark : where are we going.

devil : shut it. this is the gods department im sneaking into it. this are the angels of god they come to party in hell sometimes.

mark : what department is it.

devil : sometimes some humans are forced to do sins. innocents but unable to get out of the situations and they sin. the deed stimulator only shows the weight not the reason behind it. so god made this department for no injustice of souls. here we are.

devil gets in a cage of a sin eater.

the sin eater is sleeping in his bed. devil comes over his bed.

devil starts tickling on his chest and tits . the sineater eyes are closed and he this its a girl tickling him.

the sin eater with his eyes closed sniffs.

the sin eater :, i know this smell, hmmmmm. i know where you came from.

devil : so remeember the fragnace of hell.

after hearing a voice of a man, the sin eater geets shoocked and opens his eyes.

the sin eater : what the fuck is this. get your hands off me. [and gets

up]
devil laughs : alright my bad. i got a job for you.
the sin eater : and why do you think i will work for you.
devil laughs : if you wont, you are mine.
sin eater : what do you mean.
devil shows him th picture from his phone.
devil : i'll send this beautifull pictures to your god.
devil shows him the pictures of sin eater and transgendes with big cocks drinking and kissing.
sin eater watching and getting shocked.
devil : and then guess what happens. he throws you in hell. and i will love watching you getting boiled in a hot tub of cum. [visuals of sin eater in cum getting boiled in cum. sin eater trying to come out of the vessel but the guards pushing him back with a stick in the vesse]
sin eater : wheew you are dark.
devil : thats why people call me the devil.
sin eater : alright what do want.
devil : well, here's the kid. i want him in heaven.
sin eater : its not possible. evenn god cant decide which soul should land where. it depends on the individual.
devil : but your the sin eater.
sin eater : i can do only if the person is forced to commit a sin.
devil removes his phone : does wifi works here. my im not getting my signal.
sin eater ; alright give me his name.
devil snaps his fingers and a book falls in the hads of sineater.
the sin eater holding his file : this is your file. so thin. have you done anything in your life.
the sin eater opens his file and watching it starts laughing.
mark watching him laugh and looking at devil.
devil : cut it will you.

sin eater : i cannot help you.

devil : why?

sin eater : i have an apettite buddy. my stomach should be full from sins. [shows him his stomach] them i can help. and his sins is like a peanut for me. combining both his deeds cannot fill my appetite. im sorry. i cannot help him. maybe do the time you might reincarate into a dog. or someone might adopt you.

devil watches him.

sin eater to mark : you should have done some good things you never would had been here in the first place.

devil watches mark.

cut to

a nacked girl dancing with a rod in her hand near a nacked man tied on the log.

she is seducing him for his dick to get errect as tied man's dick gets errect. she hits it with a rod.

watching it devil laughs : haahaha right in his dick. alright bring the next one. [the man tied on the log moves and new one comes]

devil : arent you enjoying this.

mark is sitting in tense.

devil : will you learn to relax.

watchhing the next devil : who ho, what do we got here. mr. crocked teeth. [the lady starts seducing and devil watching on the laptop. and reading] let me see what have you done. chetaing, stealling, lying, adultery.

mark watches it was henry.

devil : ohh man, you got a long list of sins. and how did you die [scrolls down at the dying column of laptop] poisioned by his wife.

mark : mona. [mark completes devil's sentence by saying mona]

devil : how did you...... do you know this guy.

mark : this is the guy, is the reason im here. i never got social because

of this guy. i coould not even trust a dying man because of him. who
buried me completely. my entire life was dull because of him. did
mona kill him.
devil : yeah [starts looking into the laptop.]
devil : his wife took him to her grandmother. shhe was sick. she told
mona to bring her some medicines. and she went to the chemist to
bring her medicines. and when she came back. she saw this sheat
naked hopping on her grandmother. she went into a severe shock, she
just couldnt stand him and one night she poisioned him and he died in
his bed. [visuals henry and mark entering the grandmotthers house.
grandmoher telling mona for medicines. mona going out. mona
coming back n the house. she watches henry fucking her
grandmother. and he watches her he laughs. hots of mona tensed in
a room alone. watching him in anger. poisioning his food and henry
dying in sleep]
the girl seducing the henry shots.
mark : this is not the death he deserve.
henry's dick gets errect and she break it with her hands and henry
shouts.
devil : dont worry, im taking care of him here.
mark : no thats not enough.
mark gets up picks up the stick from the dance floor hits on henry's
teeth. and starts htiitng on his balls and devil makes weired faces.
and mark comes near the devil.
mark : whhat! i always wanted to do it and i have done it.
devil : yeah thats what im talking about. you are the new incharge
over here.
mark : i got an idea. i can sin here as much as i want and then i can
make a move.
devil : so you have made your mind to leave.
mark : come on doing same things all day. i wont do this again. i did it

when i was alive.
devil : but this is hell baby sins which you do here, wont be counted. i
think i got an idea.
cut to
devil looking for potals in his machine to enter earth.
mark : now what is going on in your evil head.
devil : looking for portals. im sending you back to earth.
mark : you are giving my life back.
devil : im only sending your soul. you go there and start sinning.
mark : can you do tha.
devil : ofcourse i can. im the devil you forgot. you come back with
bundle of bad deeds. and you will see yourself in heaven.
mark : are you serious.
devil : so select a sin. i have to curse you now. what you want to do
get possesed for muder, bombing. sperading virus. tell me your
poison.
mark : can i do sex.
devil smiles : i knew you wanted to get naughty. so i curse you that
any guy gets horny around you. that person will be possesed by you
untill you cum. good luck.
devil snaps and mark falls into a portal.
mark wakes up on the street.
mark : what a bad dream it was. huh the devil.
from the right a truck comes mark watching it shouts
the truck goes over him and he is still alive.
mark ; im still alive. ohh this means its not a dream. this means i got
lot of sex to do.
cut to
mark goes in a market.
people are walking through him. mark watches beautiful girls around
him.

mark to himself : there got to be someone horny here.
one fruit loader was loading a fruits in the truck and watches a womans cleavage.
the fruit loader : ohh the tits always turn me on.
immideatly the soul of mark gets dragged and enters the fruit loaders body.
mark to himself after getting in the body : ohhh wow, this feels good [watching his hands] so where is your prey.
mark watches the same woman and says "not bad huh"
the woman leaves from there.
other loader hits him on his head annd says " shhut the day dreaming and get back to work"
mark to himself : i guess its time to move on.
mark tries to get out of his body. but he couldnt.
mark : what the fuck is happening. then remember the devil's curse.
"person will be possesed until you cum"
mark to himself : ohhh sheat i got to cum.
mark goes in a dark road and starts jerking off and he watches himself in the window mirror. it was the fruit loader guy.
mark to himself : i dont need to jerk now. beacuse no one knows its me.
cut to
mark has catched a girl and kisses him. she kicks and runs.
then next he watches a oold woman walking . he goes there and starts doing the friction. and he cums.
as mark cums he leaves the body and the fruit loader knows nothing what happened. and he looks that he is stuck to the old lady. he leaves her. and people are gathered around him.
fruit loader : what happened.
from the crowd : i'll tell you what happened. yoou pervert.
the crowd starts beating him and the devil watching it in hell and

laughing and says ohh man this insane. and next he watches his deed calculator. ssin weight is increased.

devil : thats my boy.

cut to

mark to himself : what the fuck man. im not walking on the road again.

mark gets into a building. he watches asexy girl passing by.

mark : i wish someone gets horny here.

immediatley mark gets sucked into an appartment in a mans body.

in that apartment the man was doing gay sex.

mark gets into the tiny mans body and the other guy is huge.

mark watches himself kissing that other.

mark to the guy : no, this cant happen.

mark gets up.

the huge guy : what the fuck are you talking about.

the huge guy tries to grab the tiny guy's hand. mark pushes his hand away saying get your hands off me.

the huge guy : what are you taalking about, you brought me here.

mark : no this is mistake. im not guy who do you think i am.

the huge guy : a moment before you were craving for my cock.

mark : its hard to explain.

the huge guy gets up in anger : i"ll explain you now.

mark runs into a room and closses the door. the huge guy runs after him.

the huge guy banging the door "open the door, you do this after turning me on."

mark watching around the room. "there is no way to escape"

the huge guy banging the door. come out you little slut.

mark : what do i do. [then he gets an idea and strts removing his pants]

mark starts jerking off. "ohhh sheat its not working"

mark starts finding a posture or a picture. he finds nothing.
mark : there might some picture or posters, [he finds a gay posters.
watching it mark says "ohh fuck not this "]
mark finds a show peice doll on the table.
the huge guy as taken a axxe and breaking the door. and he watches
from the hole of the door. mark jerking off. "what the fuck are yoou
doing"
mark yellling was about to cum huh huh huuh.
cut to
shot of cum on the doll.
cut to
mark comes out.
mark to himself : fuck man it was right in my ass.
immideatly mark gets sucked into a room of old mans body. who was
on a old lady.
mark watching her ugly face. "what the fuck"
the old lady : did you came.
mark : no.
mark gets out of tthe room naked and starts running. everyone from
the floor watches him run and starts laughing.
mark runs on the roof top and starts watching a girl in a bikini from
the other building window and starts jerking off.
the girl notices him and calls the cop.
girl on phone : helo police, there is man watching me and jerking off.
police : is this a joke.
girl : no, he is right in front of me naked.
cut to
police taking the oldman out from the building.
oldman shouting : it was not me. i did nothing.
old lady : after a long time got an errection. and yoou arrest him for
that [camera panns on mark]

mark : ohh fuck i got saved

mark walking on a dark street "ohh please dont get horny, dont get horny."

one girl grabs his hand and pulls him.

mark : what the fuck.

girl is in the hood.

mark : how could you do this. you can see me.

girl removes her hood. there was a knife stuck in her head.

mark yells watching her.

girl : dont freak out. im same as you. i need your help.

mark : i need help myself, sorry girl ur knocking at the wrong door.

girl : listen to me.

mark walks away from her and looks up and says "i need your help where are you, devil whhere are you"

cut to

mark has landed hell and devil is next to him.

devil : why are you looking up im beneath the earth.

mark : i got some serious problems man.

devil : i know let me complete this [devil was doing something in laptop]

mark starts watching in to the laptop .

devil in girls voice : ohhh yes cum babby cum show me that load.

cut to

on the other sidde of the phone.

the guy from the laptop jerking and watching a girl naked on the phone. saying yes cum baby cum.

the guy comes.

cut to

devil : its so easy to get you guys.

devil watches to mark : ohhh my bad.

mark : you use internet to trap people.

devil : hey dont put this on me. [mmark and devil starst walking around the hell]
devil : people make their choices. they could have used internet for educational purposes. they chose to enter the dark web. i didnt foorce them. and everyone has their own poison. someone is greedy, some covets for beauty, someone even choose to hack and harm others. so dont blame it on me. [stops near the henry, he was getting his ass whooped]
henry : he is right .
the guard whips his ass. and henry shouts. whooo
devil : i know what happened. i just need to uprade the curse [removes his cell phone and upgrade curse]
devil : so now, you will enter a horny guy's body only if you want to and you can get out soon as he untouches the woman.
mark : why leave this way.
devil : what you want to do more. get in love, make babies and get settled down there. you are only there for sex. and dont get in love. alright get going [snaps his fingers]
mark : but i wanted to tell you i met a soul over there. [but he has reached back to earth]
mark gets in the club. and watches around. and he watchhes a couple dancing. and he looks at the girl and smiles watching her.
cut to.
the girl and the boy entering in her apartment kissing.
the girl stops kissing and holds him and says "i'll take a lleak and comes"
as she leaves him and goes towards the bathroom. the soul of mark comes out.
the guy comes in his senses : what the fuck am i doing here.
mark : you are getting me laid. just be here fuck face. what is she doing.

mark watches the girl with a knife. mark gets scared.
the girl crushes the pill with a knife and puts it in a drink.
girl comes out of the kitchen with 2 drinks. the guy was smoking.
guy : how the fuck did i get here.
girl : next you will ask, who am i.
guy looks at her. girl gives him a drink. and says this might refresh
your memory.
the guy takes the drink.
mark : no, no, dont drink it. what the fuck.
the guy drinks it. the girl kisses and watching it mark smiles and
enters his body as the girl leaves. the guy gets unconcious and falls
down.
the girl : you are not that lucky dude.
the girl comes near him and checks his pocket. suddenly the mark's
soul enters the body.
the guy opens his eyes. the girl watches him. he smiles. the girl gets
scared and she leaves removes her hand.
the guy sleeps again.
the girl again starts checking his pocket, and the guy catches her
hand, the girl watches. him and the guy smiles.
the guy : you can call me mark.
cut to
the shot of the cigerete on the hash tray and sexual sound from
behind girl shouting mark ohhh mark. and the cigerete smoke morphs
into the devils face and the devils says smoking. [song starts born to
be alive]
cut to
mark sitting in the car of the next to the drivers seat. and driver
watching the lady from the mirror. and he has hots for her.
the lady bring the lugage to my room.
driver: mam.

cut to

a make up artist doing make up to a girl. and mark is watching them both.

cut to

a girl swimming in bikini. mark is sitting behind a guy in jet ski.

cut to

the woman is having in taxi with the driver.

cut to

in a fashion show girls are walking and the camera pans behind the stage.

the make up artist is having sex with the girl.

girl : i thought you were queer.

artist : tonight you can call me mark.

cut to

the man from the jet ski and the girl kissing under water.

cut to

a celeb couple dancing together and even mark is dancing with them.

cut to

devil watching the deed calculator the sins are increasing.

cut to

the celeb woman : ohhh mark, i love you mark.

cut to

all the women on their bed are getting humped and their close up face shot. ohhh mark. you are incredible.

cut to

mark walking on the street and that same lady comes towards him.

lady : i been looking for you.

mark : please lady leave me alone, you are not suppose to be here.

lady : neither are you.

mark : i know im on a mission.

lady : its my sister. her life is in danger. you have to help her.

mark : sorry lady ttry the living, you are asking help from the dead.
[and walks away]
cut to
a man banging a girl on bed and as he is done. mark gets out, and starts walking out of the room.
mark was walking out and he hears the girl screaming. no. no, no, and the man cuts her throat. and starts grabbing her jewellery and money.
mark goes back and watches the woman is dying
mark : why did you do that.
mark : help her man, help her. she is dying
the man is busy grabbing her jewellery.
mark tries to beat him, he cant and he even tries to get back in his body. but he cant.
mark watches the girl die and the robber runs away. [song the long road, eddie vedder]
mark comes out on the street. he watches a sexy woman passing by but he ignores.
cut to
mark watching outside a guy giving food to the beggar. and the beggar getting happy.
he walks more. a man helping a blind man crossing the road.
a nurse escorting a oldman in a wheel chair.
a man giving food on the street to small children.
a man helping other guy who fell from the bike.
a man fixing a car and not taking money. and they shake hand. the guy says god bless you.
mark tries to help oldman to cross but he couldnt.
cut to
mark walking on the street and the same lady with the knife in her head comes in front of her.

mark nods his head yes.

cut to

a man in a mask beating a girl in a room tying a girl in bed . mark and the lady is watching them.

the man switches on the camera.

mark : what is this all about.

lady : he makes snuff porn, he did this with me and one day he killed me for real. and one day he gonna do same with my kid sister.

the masked guy starts beating him.

lady : please help her.

mark : i cant unless he gets horny.

lady : look he is like a satan.

mark : you know nothing about satan.

cut to

the guy tears her clothes and sits on her and mark enters his body.

mark removes her tape from the mouth.

girl : please i had enough of this.

mark : you have to listen to me very carefully. im here to help you.

girl : please your the one who is hurting me.

mark : im not the one who you think i am. i am friend of your sister.

girl : she is missing.

mark : she is dead, this same guy killed her.

girl : ohhh lord no. you are gonna kill me too.

mark to lady : how can she believe me.

lady : tell her. there was an escape plan. the money and the new passport is in the flour box.

mark : there was an escape plan. do you remember.

girl : no there was nothing.

mark : your new passport is right here, im going to untie you. you only have to trust me.

mark removes her one hand and ties on his.

lady : what are you doing.
mark : i will loose the guy if i untouch her.
girl : you are talking to who.
mark : your sister.
the girl watches on her side. : sister is that really you.
lady : yes my sweet cherry.
mark : she says i love you my sweet cherry.
unties her completely.
they take the passport and money from the flour box.
mark : do you know how to swim.
girl : yeah, but why.
they all get in the car. with the hands tied.
mark ties himself with the seat and drives. and gives her the knife.
girl : for what.
mark : when the time comes.
mark drives as a bridge comes : get your seat belts on.
lady touching the girls head : dont worry my child this will be over
soon.
car hits into the bride. and drops in to the water.
the girl removes her seat belt and unties the hand from the masked
man.
the girl swims and the masked man dies.
the girl comes out and walks and the lady says god bless you to
mark.
mark walks from there.
cut to
devil was in the his cabin joking with the other demons. and he
watches a good deed weight on the marks deeds calculator.
devil : a good deed of mark.
everyone from the room looks at him.
devil snaps his fingers and mark comes in the room.

devil : hey mark, what have you done, i have send you there to sin.
and you landed up doing good work.
mark : lets not talk about it.
devil : alright mark dont get nervous i got a surprise for you.
devil snaps the finger and there comes the boss hanging upside
down.
mark : boss.
devil : yeah your boss. a piece of sheat. you remember i didnt tell you
how you died. get a glimpe on thee night you died .
devil snaps the finger. and the big screen turns on
in the big screen.
mark coming out from his house. boss is watching him in his car and
drinking.
boss :: you bastard, want to hook my fish. just like that.
boss drives the car and runs over mark.
and boss dashes a building and runs out of the car and people are
running after him and beating him.
devil : this fellow died in jail. [boss was getting raped by gang in
shower, he fights back and gets stabbed]
devil : come on he is all yours. show little some of your moves. [acts
like boxing]
mark : do you mind if i'll get back to the punishment which i deserve.
devil stares at him and mark leaves.
boss : leave him he is always dull.
devil snaps his fingers and the boss falls into the dark room the big
dicked demon.
cut to
devil in his office with friends.
devil : let me see what happened
devil playes on big screen and everyone watching mark saved the girl.
[the song again the long road]

cut to

the guards maintaining the lineof sinners.

one guard to another : this place is getting too crowded.

other guard : humans cannot just stop sinning.

one guard : you know mark was sent back to sin. but he saved a girl.

other guard : mark who,

one guard : the jerker.

other guard : sounds like he is the nice guy.

cut to

mark is in the line of whipping. one gets it and mark comes. the guard looks at the devil and starts whipping marks back and while doing it the guard was crying and so was the devil.

devil turns and gets to his friend.

demon : come on the guy doesnt deserves this.

devil : i know.

mark is in the dark room. and devil goes there.

devil : hey mark how are you.

mark : hey my friend. how are you.

devil : stop this will you. you are hurtng me.

mark : no my friend, im getting what i deserve.

devil : you are a good chap. you got a chance and you saved a girl. . you should feel good about it.

mark : but i killed someone too.

devil : but you saved her, you want to see her.

mark looks at him .

cut to both in his office

watching the girl with her parents.

the girl and the parents pray. lord bless the soul which helped our girl back home.

in the deed calculator the blue weights increases.

devil : you see that, your a good guy, you just got your deeds raised.

devil : wait to a minute, wait a minute. i almost forgot.
mark : now what.
devil : the sin eater is just the deeds eater. everyone calls him sin
eater because. he people into heaven. cleans their slate.
mark : what are you getting at.
devil : do you remember. what the guy said.
devil snaps the finger
on the big screen. the flashback of the sin eater comes "combining
both his deeds it cannot fill my appetite"
devil snaps and the video pauses.
mark : im blank not getting anything.
devil : what the fuck man, you are the dumbest guy i have ever seen.
this means combining both your deeds can fill his appetite.
mark in confusion.
devil snaps his fingers and sin eater comes in the room with 2 she
devils.
sin eater gets hides his pecker from the pillow. and gets angry
sin eater : you just cant do this even if your a satan.
devil to girls : hi you sexy thing.
the girl says : hi.
sin eater ; whats going on here.
devil to sineater : are hungry fatso.
sin eater looks at mark
sin eater : ohh this boy. alright, lets get over with this. show me his
deeds.
devil snaps and the deed stimulator comes
devil : is this enough.
sin eater : its more than enough.
sin eater sucks the deeds and farts
everyone : whho man what ou been eating.
sin eater : say good bye, anny moment you will be gone.

mark : thank you, all this you did for me. im gonna miss you.
all the demons : we are gonna miss you too, take ccare mark, dont
jerk off in heaven. [everyone laughs]
devil : take care buddy.
mark : yeah. how will i meet youuuuuuuuuuuu ![gets in to the loop
hole]
cut to
mark opens his eyes and watches everything is white.
mark : is this really heaven.
and in front of him there is a golden gate.
angels with wings and nimbus on head opens the gate.
angels : hi mark. how was your ride.
mark starts walking in side.
mark : you know my name.
angel : yeah we do.
one angel : ohhh he is so cute.
lady : welcome to heaven.
mark : you. you are here.
lady : yeah the thing we did together. i entered the judgement gate
and here i am.
cut to
everyone says hi . even celebs are there.
lady : look go there you have to sign in in that tent..
mark starts walking towards the gods office annd there is a thumb
thing.
mark puts the thumb on the gajet and the machine answers welcome
mark.
the curtans opens and mark enters.
mmark watches a man sitting in a chair and he is facing the wall.
the name on the desk is written god.
mark to himself : ohh fuck is this is the gods cabin.

mark : sir, i mean god i came here to sign in.
the chair turns and he is the devil. but in normal skin.
god : yeah sure just put your palm there and it will done.
mark puts his hand on the desk and his hand gets scaned.
the machine says : welcome to heaven mark. now you are an member of heaven. have fun.
mark : ohhh thats awesome.
god : so how was your journey here.
mark : well it was something.
god : yeah you had a long run even after your death. first in the hell. then back to the earth, then again hell and then here. that was a big traavel plan.
mark : how do you know.
god : you think im a fool. im god. am i not. i know everything. bro
mark : you sound familiar.
god : you still didnt recognize me.
mark : no.
god snaps his fingers and turns into devil.
devil : now do you recognize me.
mark : ohh fuck. its you. man. i thought i woulld nnever see you again.
devil snaps his finger back and truns into god.
god : keep it low. no one knows. no one has ever been to both the side.
god snaps his finger and drink comes in marks hand.
god : come oon lets take a walk.
they both walking outside. the tent.
mark : so you play god here.
god : well im the god.
mark : devil in hell. so own both the places.
god : not axactly. listen i created earth and blessed humans with what ever you do you will get 10times more than it. i gave them ability to

makke earth more beautiful. instead of doing good. they decided to sin. hell was created by humans not by me. because the sins you do. you should pay for it 10 times even if you die.

mark : but you coulld have put me here anytime.

god : you still dont get it dont you. its never me. i never decide who will land where. its you. its always you. i can only show you the way. its your decision what you choose. good or evil. you choose what will happen to you. not me.

angels come ther flying.

god : ohh look the witches from salem.

mark : those are the witches.

god : they never were. thats why they got wings here.

starts calling mark.

angelS : hey new guy come along. lts party.

mark watches the angels and their tits.

mark looks at god : may i.

god : ooffcourse you can.[mark starts walking in exitment] this is heaven. you can do anything you like.

god : hey mark, dont you tell my secret.

mark : dont you worry i just cant wait to....[mark goes near the angels puts his hand on their shoulders. "so tell me girls what is the coolest place here."]

angel : the waterfall, garden.

mark : well we will see them one by one.

god watching mark going with the angels.

god turns back to the audiance.

god : ohh you guys, look mark got a chance to be in heaven. i dont think you will be that lucky. so i starts doing the good work.

god snaps and turns into the devil.

devil : or i will be waiting for you in the hell [and smiles]

this doesnt ends here, there wiill be a new version of afterlife. the part 2 will be coming soon with more fun . written by yogendra niikale, this is a raw script version but the real version of book will come out soon.

Contents